I LOVE YOU
JUST THE WAY YOU ARE

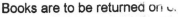

Virginia Miller

WALKER BOOKS
AND SUBSIDIARIES
LONDON • BOSTON • SYDNEY

One day Bartholomew was grumpy…
His ears were cold.

"Wrap your scarf around your ears
to keep them warm," said George.

But Bartholomew was still grumpy.
His legs felt too stumpy.

"I'll carry you," said George.

At home, Bartholomew's porridge was too lumpy,

his tummy too plumpy,

and he was too small.

"I'll feed you," said George.

At bathtime, Bartholomew hid.

He did not like **anything** at **all**.

"What a day," said George.
"You've been so grumpy,
  your legs have felt stumpy,
  your porridge too lumpy,
  your tummy too plumpy
      but Ba ..."

"I love you
just the way you are."

Bartholomew felt better. He kissed George,

and brushed his teeth all by himself.

"Time for bed, Ba," said George.
"We both need a little rest."

"Nah," said Bartholomew.